Yawning is Catc

Workshopped by Beverley Burkett, Denise Manning
Lungi Radasi and Lyn Stonestreet

Illustrated by Lyn Stonestreet

CAMBRIDGE
UNIVERSITY PRESS

Baby Busi lay near the river
while her mother worked in the fields.

A frog hopped up and saw Baby Busi.

"Kwaak! Kwaak! Kwaak! 1–2–3!
A plump little baby all for me!"

The frog opened his mouth wide and *gulped* down Baby Busi.

And hop, hop, hop went the frog down to the river.
But before he reached the river he met a snake!
"Sssss! Sssss! Sssss! 1-2-3!
A fat little frog all for me!"

The snake opened her mouth wide and *gulped* down the frog.

And slither, slither, slither went the snake down to the river.
But before she reached the river she met a tall bird!

"Skree! Skree! Skree! 1-2-3
A slippery little snake all for me!"

The tall bird opened his beak wide and *gulped* down the snake.

And flap, flap flap went the tall bird down to the river.
But before he reached the river he met a crocodile!
"Snap! Snap! Snap! 1-2-3
A juicy big bird all for me!"

The crocodile opened her mouth wide and *gulped* down the tall bird.

And she slipped into the river.

A big hippo was lazing in the water.
He opened his big mouth and yawned.
It was a very, very big yawn. *Yaaaaaaaah!*

And what happens when you see someone yawning?
You yawn too! *Yaaaaaaaah!* Yawning is catching!
The crocodile saw the hippo yawning.
And guess what happened?

Crocodile yawned a great big yawn. *Yaaaaaaaah!*
And *out* flapped the bird!

The bird saw the crocodile yawning
and the bird yawned a great big yawn. *Yaaaaaaaah!*

And *out* slithered the snake!

The snake saw the bird yawning
and the snake yawned a great big yawn. *Yaaaaaaaah!*

And *out* hopped the fat frog!

The frog saw the snake yawning
and the frog yawned a great big yawn. *Yaaaaaaaah!*

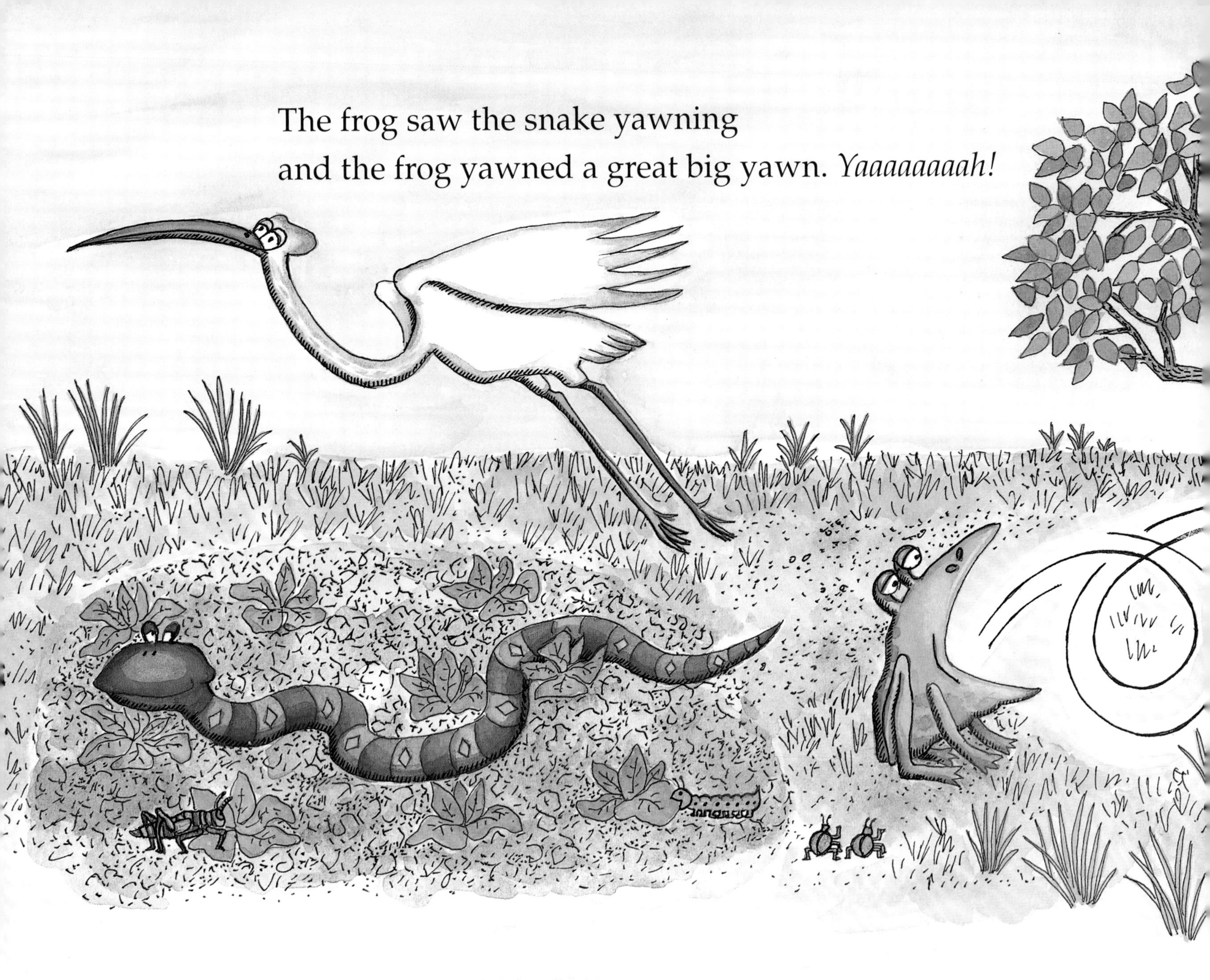

And *out* popped Baby Busi!

She landed right back on her blanket under the tree.
At that moment Busi's mother came back.
She bent down and smiled at Baby Busi.
"Have you had a good sleep?" she asked.

Baby Busi just yawned a great, big, happy yawn!

Yaaaawn!

Judo

Neil Adams MBE

Contents

Photography by Bob Willingham

The publishers would like to thank all those who gave their assistance in making this book, especially Lee Burbridge, Matthew Lewis, Nicola Lewis, Andy Smith, and David Somerville.

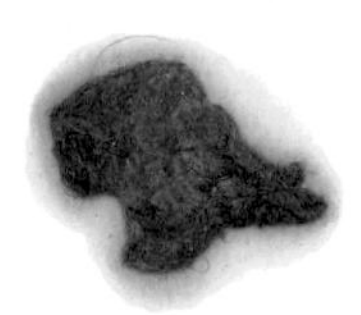

INTRODUCING JUDO

Judo is a sport which started in Japan more than 100 years ago. Now it is played and enjoyed in many different countries by people of all ages.

The name judo is a Japanese word meaning 'the gentle way'. It is a form of fighting or wrestling in which one player can beat another but in such a way that no one gets hurt. The two opponents use the skills they learn to try to throw each other to the ground and hold their rival down. It is played on thick mats which act like a cushion so that it does not hurt when a player is thrown.

Judo is growing in popularity and top-level competitions attract lots of spectators.

How judo started

The man who invented judo was called Jigoro Kano. As a young man, Kano studied **ju-jitsu**. This was an old form of Japanese self-defence. It was dangerous as you could hit your opponent with your hands, feet or elbows. It also included moves to force an opponent's arm or leg joints the wrong way to inflict pain.

Jigoro Kano thought that it was important for schoolboys to learn about Japanese ways of hand-to-hand fighting. He knew that a safer form of fighting was needed if it was to be taught in Japanese schools. Judo is his safe form of fighting.

The difference between judo and ju-jitsu is that no blows or kicks are allowed in judo so it can be practised safely.

The Olympic Games

As judo became known outside Japan and interest in the new sport spread, judo clubs were formed. The first judo contests were held between clubs. Then came national and, finally, international competitions. In 1964 judo became an Olympic sport for men.

In the early days ladies were only allowed to learn some basic judo movements, called '**katas**'. Eventually judo became accepted as a sport for ladies too. At the 1992 Olympic Games, ladies' judo will be included for the first time.

The sport was first seen in Britain about 100 years ago when some Japanese players came to Europe to demonstrate judo skills.

The language of judo

Judo comes from Japan, so many of the words used in the sport are Japanese. Where Japanese words are used in this book they will be shown the first time in heavy type like this: **katas**.

Judo today is played by both girls and boys.

JUDO KIT

The kit judo players wear is called **judo-gi**. It consists of a white jacket and trousers made from very strong cotton material and tied with a belt.

The jacket:
It should be big enough to cross over, left over right, by at least 20cm.

The correct sleeve length is between the wrist joint and 5cm above it.

The belt:
It must be long enough to go round you twice with enough left to tie in a knot.

The colour shows what level of player you are. (See page 6)

The trousers:
The correct length is between the ankle joint and 5cm above it.

How to tie your belt

1. Put the belt round your waist, keeping the two ends equal.

2. Cross the ends over behind you and bring them round to the front.

3. Cross the left end over the right. Pull it up, under *both* layers of the belt.

4. Pass the right end over the left. Pull it up through the gap to finish the knot.

Footwear

Judo is played barefoot. But to get to and from the mat area, you must wear shoes in order to keep the mat clean.

Special judo slippers are called zori

Safety tips:

- Do not wear watches or jewellery as they can cause injury or get broken.
- Keep fingernails and toenails cut short so you will not scratch other players.
- Tie long hair out of the way so that it does not swing and lash you and so that you can see properly.

JUDO GRADES AND BELT COLOURS

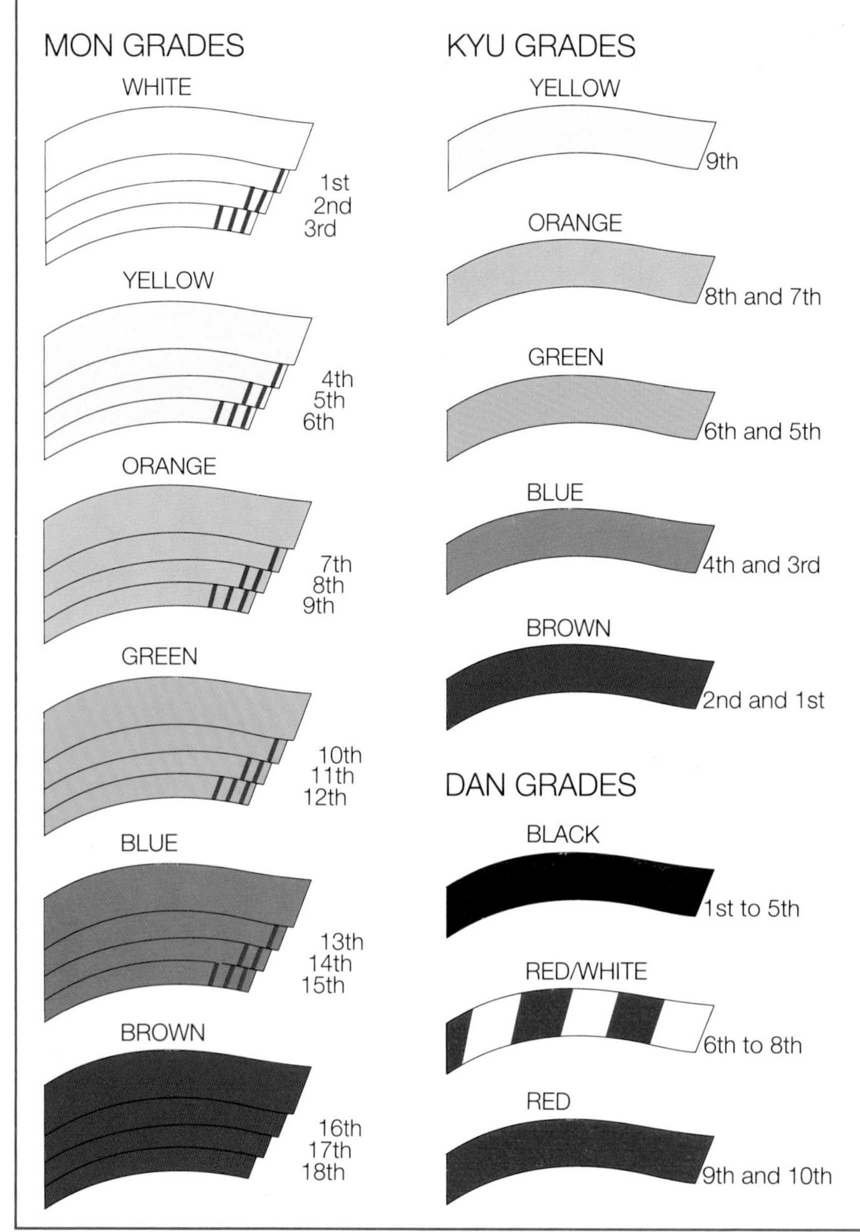

The colour of your belt shows what level of judo player you are. The colour grades shown here are used by the British Judo Association and are recognised all over the world.

For players less than 16 years old there are 18 grades, called **mons**. There are six belt colours and each colour is divided into three levels. The levels are shown with 1, 2, or 3 red stripes sewn onto one end of your belt. When you are 16 years old you change over to senior grades, called **kyu**. The colour of your belt when you become a senior depends what level you reached as a junior player. When you have reached 1st kyu you can begin to work for the **dan** grades.

FIRST THINGS FIRST

Once you have decided that you want to become a judo player, or **judoka**, you will need to find a class or club to join. Look at the notice board at the local sports centre or public library to see what classes are advertised. If you write to the British Judo Association (see page 32) they will send you a list of clubs in your area. Then go along and watch a class.

In the class

The room where you do your judo training is called the **dojo**. In the dojo, most of the floor is covered by thick rubber matting. All judo practice takes place on this padded surface.

First class

At first, your teacher will take everything very slowly. Watch and listen carefully. Try to remember what you are shown.

In the first lesson, you will probably learn about some of the customs of judo, like bowing to your teacher and the other judoka. Then you will start learning different ways to fall and roll on the mat without hurting yourself. These are called breakfalls and are some of the first skills you will learn. Once you have mastered these you will be ready to start learning the different ways to throw an opponent.

Bowing

Japanese people bow to each other when they meet or say goodbye, a bit like our custom of shaking hands. In the dojo you bow to show respect to your teacher and your opponents.

The standing bow is made to your opponent before and after each contest, even when you are only practising.

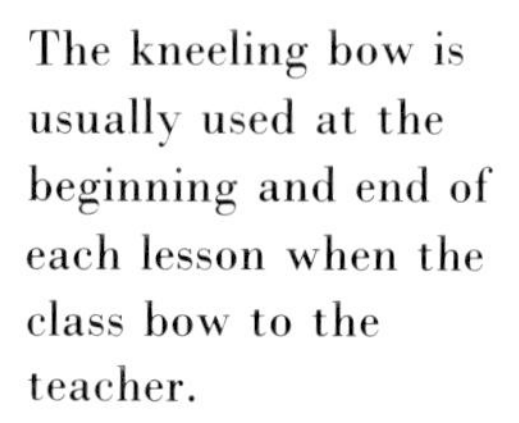

The kneeling bow is usually used at the beginning and end of each lesson when the class bow to the teacher.

Warming up

The class often starts with simple exercises like running, stretching and rolling. These are to get you moving and 'warm up' your muscles and joints so you will not hurt yourself when you come to try some of the movements later in the lesson. Here are some warm-up exercises for you to try.

Hip rotation

Stand up straight with your feet apart. Put your hands on your hips. Push your hips out to the right, then swing them round to the back, then to your left and back to the front. Try and make the whole circle into one smooth movement. Circle your hips to the right 10 times then try it to the left.

Armswings

Stand up straight with your feet apart. Lift both arms up above your head and swing them forwards in a big circle. Try this 10 times. Then try swinging them backwards 10 times. Now try swinging one arm at a time; 10 times forwards then 10 times backwards.

Running on the spot

Spring from one foot to the other and pump your arms like you do when running normally but bring your knees up high in front of you.

Start slowly and see if you can keep running like this for 2 minutes. Keep your back straight, head up and relax your shoulders. Look straight ahead.

BREAKFALLS

Learning to fall so that you do not hurt yourself is one of the first skills you will learn. These movements are sometimes practised as part of the warm-up at the beginning of the class. In each case, you do not just hit the mat and stop. Instead you tuck up and roll on the mat and slap the mat with your arm and palm of your hand to take the force out of the fall.

Side breakfall

Squat on the mat. Choose which way you are going to fall. (To the right in this example.)

Swing your left arm and leg out sideways so that you topple to the right. As you fall stretch out your right arm and slap the mat with the palm of your hand.

Backward breakfall

Squat on the mat and hold your arms out in front to balance. Tuck your chin down on your chest.

Keep your back rounded and let yourself roll back. Slap both hands, palms down, on the mat as your back touches it. Keep your chin tucked in so your head does not hit the mat.

Forward roll with breakfall

Step one foot forward and bend your front knee. Tuck your chin into your chest and lean forward.

With the same arm forward, as leg, let yourself fall into a forward roll, tucked into a ball. Keep your arm and shoulder curved.

As you come out of the roll, slap the mat with your free hand.

Rolling breakfall with a partner.

Kneel on your hands and knees and pass one hand under your tummy. Let your partner take a firm hold of your hand.

Your partner will pull that arm and push on your other shoulder to flip you over onto your back. Break the force of the fall by stretching out your free arm and slapping the mat with the palm of your hand.

Practice tip:

- Most people find it easier to fall to one side than the other. Make sure you practise both ways and don't always use the same arm or leg.

Once you have learnt the basic skills of falling you are ready to practise breakfalls in a proper throwing situation.

TYPES OF THROW

There are three basic types of throw: forwards, backwards, and sideways, and for each there are lots of different ways to throw your opponent. Some throws may look the same but look again and you will see that the players use different hand holds or foot positions.

Every throw has three stages to it.
1) the entry (the way you approach)
2) the throw
3) the exit (the way you finish)

All throws are easier to do when you are moving but to learn a new throw you will start by standing still. Then you have to walk through each stage in slow motion. Your teacher will check that you are doing it correctly. Then you will have to repeat the throw many times until you can do it without thinking and it looks as if you are doing all three stages in one easy action.

Attacking and defending

The name for the attacker is **tori**. The defender is called **uke**. In class you will take it in turns to be tori and uke so that you learn how to attack an opponent and how to defend yourself. In a competition, of course, both judoka want to be tori because they can score points for attacking moves (see page 29).

FORWARD THROWS – TACHI WAZA

Tachi waza means standing techniques. It describes forward, backward and side throws. You can make a forward throw standing on two feet or you can balance on one leg using the other one to sweep uke's legs away. If you use a sweeping throw you must make sure that you keep control of your opponent throughout the throw.

Ippon seoi nage

1. Tori pins uke's arm by putting his right arm under uke's armpit and takes hold of uke's sleeve or lapel.

2. Tori turns his right hip into uke. He leans slightly forward, keeping his back straight and bending his knees.

3. He straightens his knees, lifting uke off-balance and turns her over with a strong pulling action on her sleeve.

Morote seoi nage

1. Tori (on the right) takes hold of uke's sleeve and lapel. She steps forward, between uke's feet, and turns.

2. As tori's right elbow bends, she pushes it up into uke's armpit. Her knees bend, ready for the throw.

3. Tori leans forward and straightens her knees. She pulls with her left hand and pushes with her right to throw uke to the mat.

Tai otoshi

In this throw, tori's feet stay on the outside of uke's legs.

1. Tori steps his right foot across, and bends his knees to lift uke off-balance.

2. He pulls on uke's sleeve and pushes with the lapel hand to finish the throw.

Harai goshi

1. Tori steps her left leg between uke's feet.

2. Tori turns on her left foot and bends that knee. Her right leg sweeps uke's leg so he begins to fall.

3. Tori straightens her left knee, and with a strong pulling action on uke's sleeve, finishes the throw.

Uchi mata

1. This throw starts like harai goshi. Tori takes a firm grip and places his left foot between uke's legs.

2. Tori turns on his left foot and bends his left knee. This time his right leg sweeps inside uke's legs.

3. Tori pulls hard with his left hand and pushes with his right hand to turn uke over and on to the mat.

BACKWARD THROWS – TACHI WAZA

Like forward throws, there are many different backward ones. Here you can see the four basic backward throws which form the base for all the other variations.

All the backward moves shown are made by balancing on one leg and using the other one to hook or sweep away uke's legs

Osoto gari

1. As soon as tori has gripped uke, by the sleeve and lapel, he steps forward on his left foot and hooks his right leg round uke's leg.

2. Tori sweeps his right leg back, taking uke's feet off the ground. At the same time he uses his hands to control uke.

3. Tori pushes uke down onto the mat and holds him there, ready to carry on fighting on the ground.

O uchi gari

1. Tori steps on to his left foot, turns his right hip quickly towards uke and hooks his right leg strongly round uke's left leg.

2. Tori then sweeps uke's left leg away with his right leg.

3. At the same time he pushes uke on to his back, ready to pin him down on the mat.

Ko uchi gari

1. Tori sweeps his right leg forwards and hooks uke's right leg away.

2. Tori moves forward and pushes uke backwards with force.

3. Tori controls the throw with his hands all the way, until uke is pinned down.

Kosoto gari

1. Tori (on the left) uses his right leg to hook uke's left leg away.

2. As tori falls forward, the movement drives uke backwards.

3. Tori now follows into ground work.

Combining two throws

A backward throw can be used to put uke off balance so that tori has the chance to make a major forward throw. Here is a o uchi gari followed by an ippon seoi nage.

1. Tori (on the right) steps on to his right foot, turns his left hip towards uke. He hooks his left leg inside uke's right leg.

2. As uke's right leg is hooked away, uke loses his balance and starts to push forward. Tori then makes the change.

3. He turns quickly, letting go with his right hand. He gets his right arm under uke's armpit and bends his knees.

4. Tori lifts uke off balance and starts turning him over with a strong pulling action on his right sleeve.

5. Tori controls the throw with his hands right through the final stages of the throw, and uke is on the mat.

Practice tips:

- Check each stage is correct, then practise over and over again.
- Practise all the skills to your right side and to your left, equally.

SIDE THROWS – ASHI WAZA

Ashi waza means foot and ankle techniques in Japanese. Some people find these the most difficult type of throws to learn. This is because the timing of each stage of the throw has to be very precise if it is to succeed.

De ashi barai (one foot sweep)

This skill can be used when both judoka are moving sideways. The attack is made as the judoka move closer together.

Tori (on the right) uses his right leg to sweep uke's advanced left foot away. At the same time he uses his hands to control uke down on to the mat.

Okuri ashi barai (two foot sweep)

This is a variation of de ashi bạri. As before, both judoka are moving but this time tori uses his right leg to sweep both of uke's feet away.

Blocking ankle techniques

Sweeping your opponents feet away is one way of throwing uke. Another way is to block the ankle or leg that uke is standing on and then force uke to overbalance. It is important for tori to co-ordinate the action so that tori does not kick uke's legs.

Sasae tsuri komi ashi

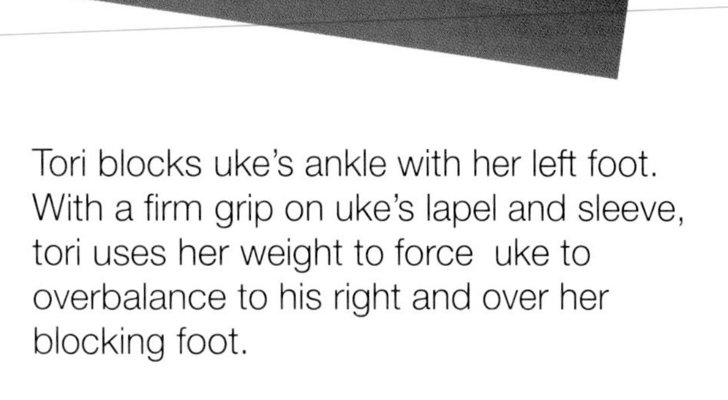

Tori blocks uke's ankle with her left foot. With a firm grip on uke's lapel and sleeve, tori uses her weight to force uke to overbalance to his right and over her blocking foot.

Hiza guruma (knee wheel)

1. For this blocking throw, both judoka have to move round each other. Tori (on the right) takes his grip on uke and starts walking round uke clockwise. This forces uke to move round.

2. When they are moving, tori (now on the left) uses his right foot to block uke's left leg. Tori uses the speed of the turning movement and strong hand movements to throw uke forcefully.

Tori blocks uke's leg at knee-level. This movement gives the throw its name.

GROUND HOLDS – NE WAZA

Ne waza means ground work. If a throw has not scored the maximum points possible (see page 29) play carries on and becomes ground fighting. Points can be scored by pinning uke down on his or her back.

It is not easy to hold an opponent down. To succeed you must control uke's head and keep chest-to-chest contact all the time. You must also take care not to let your legs become tangled up with uke's legs or your ground hold will not count.

Kesa gatame

Kesa gatame means 'scarf hold'. Tori puts his right arm round uke's neck (like a scarf) and takes hold of uke's collar.

This pins uke's left arm. Tori spreads his legs apart to help keep him in a strong position when uke struggles.

Yoko shiho gatame

Yoko in Japanese means side. This hold is a very strong one and one of the most popular. Tori's arm goes around uke's head and he grips the lapel. Tori's head and chest lie across uke's chest. He passes his free arm between uke's legs and takes hold of uke's belt. All the time he keeps his legs spread apart for stability.

Kami shiho gatame

In this hold, tori controls the upper part of uke's body. Tori's head and chest lie over uke's chest. Tori passes both his hands under uke's arms and takes hold of uke's belt either side.

Tate shiho gatame

Tori sits on uke and wraps both legs round the upper part of uke's legs. He crosses his feet to prevent uke escaping. This controls uke's legs. Tori lies across uke's chest, trapping one of uke's arms up, and this secures the hold.

Body contact exercise

Here is an exercise for you to try with a partner. Start by lying across your partner from the side. Your partner should struggle slightly while you work your way round his head to the other side. Make sure you keep chest-to-chest contact and pin your partner down all the time.

PLAYING JUDO

Once you have learnt the basic skills of breakfalling and just a few judo techniques you can begin to play competitive judo. At first, this will just be part of your practice in class. There, you will learn what you must do to score and the rules of the game. Then you might start competing against other members of your club. As you get more experienced your club may arrange competitions against another club.

The mat area in which the contest takes place is clearly marked in red. At a large competition several contests take place at the same time.

The mat area

In a judo competition, the contest takes place in a large square marked on the mat. The square must be at least 14m x 14m but no larger than 16m x 16m. The edge is marked by a red line, 1m wide. This is called the danger area. If either judoka goes into the danger area and stays there for more than 5 seconds, penalty points will be given. If both judoka accidently go outside the mat area, the contest is stopped. Then, both players go back into the centre and the contest can continue.

The contestants

The players wear either a red or a white belt round their jackets. This is to help the referee to tell them apart in the confusion of fast and furious play.

The red or white competition belts are worn over the player's normal belt.

Contest time

The contest time for junior players is 4 minutes. Senior players fight for 5 minutes. This is actual fighting time. If the contest is stopped, for example when the players accidently go outside the mat area, the clock is stopped too. The clock is restarted when the players have been brought back into the centre.

If these judoka go outside the mat area, this contest will be stopped and they will have to go back into the centre to carry on fighting.

The referee and line judges

The contest is controlled by a referee. His job is to make sure that the contest is fought within the rules of the game and the scores are correctly recorded. The referee is helped by two line judges. They stand on opposite corners of the mat area where they can see if there is any foul play on the mat edge. If both judges agree to a score which is different to the one given by the referee, they can overrule him. If both judges and the referee all give different scores, the referee has to take the middle value score. And if there is no score, the judges show who they think should win, and the referee makes the final decision.

The scores are displayed on electronic scoreboards. So far, neither player has scored in this contest.

The line judges have to be prepared to move out of the contestants way.

How to score

The main aim in judo is to score an **ippon**. An ippon scores 10 points and wins the contest. For players under 16 years old, there are two ways in which to score. One way is to throw your opponent on to the mat. The other is to pin your opponent on the mat using one of the recognised groundholds. How many points you score depends how well you do either of these two things. The table below shows the four possible scores and what you have to do to achieve them.

Score	Throwing Tachi waza	Holding Ne waza
Ippon 10 points	Throw an opponent with reasonable force on to their back	Hold an opponent on their back for 30 seconds
Waza ari 7 points	Throw an opponent almost on to their back	Hold an opponent on their back for 25 seconds
Yuko 5 points	Throw an opponent on to part of their back with less force than above	Hold an opponent on their back for 20 seconds
Koka 3 points	Trip an opponent so they fall on to any part of their back or rear	Hold an opponent on their back for 10 seconds

Two waza ari scores = one ippon.

- *Only* waza ari points can be added together to make a higher score.
- If no ippon is scored, the referee and judges will award the contest to the player with the highest single score. For example, a player with one yuko will beat a player with ten kokas.

What is against the rules?

Penalty points will be given when you break the rules in a competition. Here are some of the most common offences.

- stepping out of the mat area on purpose
- pushing your opponent outside the mat area
- spending too much time in the red danger area
- crawling out of the mat area
- not attacking at least every 20 seconds
- adopting a very defensive posture
- running away or avoiding your opponent
- time wasting
- punching, pinching, biting or kicking
- swearing
- applying pressure to your opponent's face
- doing any throw or hold that is judged to be dangerous to either fighter

The speed of play in today's big contests can make it difficult for the referee and judges to reach a decision. Video recordings are sometimes used to help.

PENALTY POINTS		
Shido	3 points	This is given for minor offences such as not attacking your opponent enough.
Chui	5 points	A more severe penalty given for offences such as bad edge play.
Keikoku	7 points	This is a severe penalty, usually given for offences which are judged to be dangerous.
Two **keikoku** penalties = **honosoku maki** which means disqualification		

Enjoy your judo

Now you know just a little bit about the exciting sport of judo. You can see what fun it is and you can see some of the basic skills that you will learn. But this is only the beginning, and you cannot learn such a physical activity from a book.

For each of the skills shown here, there are hundreds of different ways of doing them, and enough advanced skills and tactics to keep you learning for a lifetime.

But, first things first, now is the time for you to become a real judoka. So, if you have not already done so, choose a club to join and start playing judo.

INDEX

First published in Great Britain 1992
Reprinted 1993

A CIP catalogue record for this book is available from the British Library.

ISBN: 0 00 191324-7 Hardback
0 00 191325-5 Paperback

Set in 12/14 Helvetica
Printed and bound in Hong Kong

AUTHOR'S ACKNOWLEDGEMENT

A special thank you to Alison, my wife, for all her help and support.

For a list of judo clubs in your area, write, enclosing a self-addressed and stamped envelope to:

THE BRITISH JUDO ASSOCIATION
7a Rutland Street
Leicester LEI IRB.